John Todhunter

Alcestis

A Dramatic Poem

John Todhunter

Alcestis
A Dramatic Poem

ISBN/EAN: 9783337158323

Printed in Europe, USA, Canada, Australia, Japan

Cover: Foto ©Andreas Hilbeck / pixelio.de

More available books at **www.hansebooks.com**

ALCESTIS:

A DRAMATIC POEM.

BY

JOHN TODHUNTER,

AUTHOR OF "LAURELLA, AND OTHER POEMS.

"Still, since one thing may have so many sides,
I think I see how—far from Sophokles—
You, I, or any one might mould a new
Admetos, new Alkestis."—*Balaustion's Adventure.*

LONDON:

C. KEGAN PAUL & CO., 1 PATERNOSTER SQUARE.

1879.

PREFACE.

It is, perhaps, scarcely necessary to say that "Alcestis" is not in any manner intended as an imitation of the Greek drama, the lyrical passages which occur being merely ornaments, not essentially connected with the action. My aim has been to write an English, not a pseudo-Greek play.

The plot being a "free fantasia" upon the prehistoric legend, I have not been solicitous about an accurate delineation of the manners and customs of any historic period. My Thessaly is the Arcadian region of a Greece almost as purely ideal as Shakespeare's Bohemia, or Forest of Arden; and to the sympathetic reader's imagination I trust the frank anachronism between modern sentiments and their legendary setting.

DRAMATIS PERSONÆ.

ADMETUS, King of Thessaly.

ALCESTIS, his wife.

PHERES, his father.

HERCULES.

EUPHRANOR, Chief-Priest of Apollo.

ŒNANTHUS, Steward to Admetus.

EUMELUS, }
CLYMENE, } Children of Admetus.

ÆGLE, a Thessalian Maiden.

A PRIEST OF APOLLO.

A CITIZEN.

A SAILOR.

Chorus of Youths and Maidens; Chorus of Mourners; Pheræans, Servants, &c.

The scene is laid in the City of Pheræ, except in Act I. Scene 2, in which it shifts to the southern border of Thessaly.

The action occupies nearly four entire days, *i.e.*, from sunrise on the first to past midnight on the fourth. About three days elapse between the First and Second Acts.

ALCESTIS.

—◆----

ACT I.

Scene I.—Pheræ—A Public Place. A crowd assembled. A band of youths and maidens preparing for the festival of Apollo. A march.

[*Enter* Admetus *and* Alcestis, *attended.*

YOUTHS (*strewing laurel*).

Hail, great Admetus !

MAIDENS (*strewing myrtle*).

Fair Alcestis, hail !

BOTH.

All hail, beloved life of this our land !
Our head and heart, on this glad day, all hail!

ADMETUS.

Thanks, gentle friends.

A

ALCESTIS.

We thrive upon your love.

ADMETUS.

Where is our laurel-bearer?

A YOUTH.

Here, my Lord!

ADMETUS.

Come to the front.   And you, fair girls, whose throats,
Nature's white organ-pipes, look beautiful
With their yet-voiceless music, after him
Marshal your virgin ranks; the shawms behind.
So—wait my signal.   We'll enrich the day
With our glad hymns.   How swells my heart, Alcestis,
This long-expected morn!   Looks not the god
From his bliss-flaming car, whose radiance fills
The crystal courts of dawn, and drinks its mist
From the blue deep, with most auspicious eye
Upon our rites.   This day I live indeed!

ALCESTIS.

What did'st thou yesterday?

ADMETUS.

　　　　　　　　I crawled till now
O'er the rude field of life, a careful grub,
Gathering the food of greatness ; but to-day
Achievement's wings, bursting their larval shell,
Flash in the dew of the morn.

ALCESTIS.

　　　　　　　O far, and high,
And happy be their flight ! But cheapen not
The worth of our lived lives—the toils, the dangers,
The woes, despairs, defeats, that we have known,
And made so dear by sharing.   That fair past,
Bought with our deedful days, is all our own,
The unpurchased future slave to no man's power.

ADMETUS.

I have no quarrel with the past, yet praise it
But as the past.   The future's sunny peak,
Spied through its cloudy climbing, fills my gaze
With forward-looking joy.

ALCESTIS.

　　　　　　　Ah ! dear, the gods,
Who love us best, give not their gifts for nought—
They must be paid twice over.

ADMETUS.

Once with sorrow—
That's done, so now with joy. Therefore rejoice,
And pay them! Grace my triumph with the light
Of thy sweet face, that healed with tenderest hope
My day of failure, and I'm thewed more strong
To grapple with prosperity's evil brood,
Dangerous to-day, than when I fronted first
Life's perilous forehead ; stronger by ten lives
Than even ten years ago, when—thou rememberest ?
I tamed for thee, to draw thy nuptial car,
The lion and the bull. We have tamed since then
The earth, my Queen, and men more fell than beasts.

ALCESTIS.

In prime my brother. 'Twas a gentle deed—
Acastus needed taming. Yes, in sooth,
Those were sad years—those wars.

ADMETUS.

Two ghastly years
Of foolish war, to tear thee from me ! Well,
They bound us all the tighter, thee and me ;
And for Acastus' self his own defeat
Was nobler victory. We triumphed then
Not vainly o'er his arms but o'er his heart.

ALCESTIS.

Those wars were in Apollo's years.

ADMETUS.

Ay, still
The glorious god by our Thessalian streams
Pastured my breeding flocks.   In those rude times
He made our little nook of the jarring world
Like a close wood that shrouds the nightingale
When tempest rends the heaven ; or as a dell
A glow-worm's lamp charms from the waste of night.

ALCESTIS.

He sang us golden songs.

ADMETUS.

He taught me wisdom,
Sweet as the Muses' singing, when their feet
Wander among the brooks and cloistered pines
Of Helicon ; so sweet that in my soul,
It kindled hopes undying.   While my ear
Holds its faint echoes even, I shine full-armed
In tranquil power—all great and glorious things
Seem possible for the world.   Thou knowest how often
To my care-weighted pillow sleep has brought
Some virtuous word of it, for joy whereof
I have waked wondering.

ALCESTIS.

        Are thy dreams not mine,
Even as thine own?

ADMETUS.

        Thou art my wife indeed,
Dearer than life-blood.   Well, thy king of dreams
Looks to thee now for his ambition's crown;
And with glad cheer I ask thy aid to-day,
To hold in mirth this sovran festival—
This dream come true.   How long have we aspired
Yon ten-years-building temple of the god
To consecrate; to hear his oracle
Speak from the cavern cloven by the stroke
Of that caducean rod he drove our flocks
To pasture with, ere from his glorious hand,
In payment for the lyre, dark Hermes took it,
To drive the dead in Hades!

ALCESTIS.

        I am thine
In triumph as defeat.

ADMETUS.

        Have I not loved
Before all gods Apollo and the Nine;

Served them with genial rites ; sequestered them
A garden from the wilderness of the world,
And taught all climes their worship?   Io Pæan !
Bright Pythian, am I not become thy lyre,
And what barbarian hand shall rend my strings ?

ALCESTIS.

Thou hast indeed in this rough world wrought wonders ;
So great that sometimes—pardon me, sweet love,
Such word on such a day ; my love, that yearns
To be thy glory's shield, creates perchance
Its visionary fears where none should cry—
But sometimes I have feared the jealousy
Of Zeus himself.

ADMETUS.

The wrath of Zeus?   There speaks the core of thy fear?
O for twelve years of life, and let him blast me
With all his thunderbolts, my work shall stand,
And mortals bless my name !

ALCESTIS.

                    Ah ! dear Admetus,
Tempt not his wrath.   Think on the piteous fate
Of demi-gods he hath struck.   Apollo's self
Could but avenge, not save, his mighty son,

The healer Æsculapius.   Other gods
Live in the mutable world than bright Apollo,
And brook not slighting.   Think how oft his peers
Have filled with tears of rage his radiant eyes,
Bacchus for Orpheus, Zeus for Phaethon,
And other griefs he hath borne.

ADMETUS.

                    Twelve years of life,
To outdo my dreams, and I'll defy the thunder.
But I have honoured Zeus and all the gods ;
They have no cause for jealousy.   Come, my love,
Give to festivity thy ill-boding heart,
And doom me life to-day, if death to-morrow.
Come ; the great image, where our fostering god
Lives, breathes and moves in gold and ivory,
A flame of glorious youth, a joy, a terror,
A power to save or slay—so cunningly
The dædal hand of Cresilas hath carved
The vision of his soul—awaits unveiling ;
And then thou shalt behold such gracious games,
Such wrestling, running, whirling the swift disc,
Such ardent striving of our beauteous youth,
That thou wilt say we have peopled Thessaly
With demi-gods ; and after thou shalt hear
Nine laurelled bards, the best of Greece, contend,
Singing the fate of Linus, lyre against lyre.

ALCESTIS.

Our songtide swells to its rich May.   I have heard
Glycon shall have the vote.

ADMETUS.

                         The women love him,
And plot his crowning ; but our old Chrysippus,
His eyes aglow with an immortal fire,
Vows to outsing himself.   'Twill be rare singing.
Come then !   How, as we move, the people's smile
Follows us still, as sunflowers seek the light.
This is to be a king !   Trust me, Alcestis,
I do believe that were my life at pawn,.
The meanest here would give his own in fee,
To ransom me.

ALCESTIS.

                         That were bare duty in him ;
Yet death's a dreadful word—a dreadful word,
Even for the wretch who drags his load of pain
Through the world's weary places.   How much more
For men whom thou hast given the wine of life
To drink in many a comfortable cup !
Will they give back thy gifts ?
                    [*The sun becomes gradually darkened.*

VOICES IN THE CROWD.

Alas! a portent!

ADMETUS.

What mean these cries? What stirs the wavering crowd,
That they turn pale and stare?

ALCESTIS.

O, my dear Lord,
Look what a shade eats up the bounteous sun!
The light of Hades dims the fields; the flocks
Huddle together trembling; the scared birds
Fly wild; the lark drops like a plummet, dumb;
The hawk cowers like the sparrow! What is this?
O, if Zeus arms to smite thee, clasp me close,
And let us stand one undistinguished mark
For his stern thunder!

ADMETUS.

Nay, my dearest love,
Comfort thy fluttering heart. I fear no evil.
O men of Pheræ! wherefore stand ye so,
With knees that knock each other? Shame upon you!
O fearful herds, not men, where are your souls;
Your human magnanimity, that should keep

Its balanced calm, though heaven came ruining down,
And all the gods, riding the thunderstorm,
Should threaten earth with chaos !   Learn to die,
When die ye must, with such heroic grace
As fits the victor in some glorious game,
And have the gods for praisers.   Here's no dying,
Though darkness comes ere noon.   Ye dread no ill,
When night by night Apollo's fiery steeds
Plunge in the western wave, and stable there,
In the cerulean caverns of the deep,
To wake renewed next morn; and there's a cave
In the blue fields of heaven, where, year by year,
Leaving his stithy in the nether glooms,
Hephæstus forges for the Lord of Day
His golden chariot-wheels.   What wonder then
That on this sacred morn his chariot pauses
A moment in that cave, while those swift hands
Fix the far-flashing fellies?   Wait awhile,
And ye shall mark that radiant car come forth
In twofold brightness.   Come, reform your ranks !
We'll hail it with a hymn, then to the temple.

                    [*Enter* A PRIEST OF APOLLO.

What bodes this pale vancourier of fate ?
Speak thy news low, as for my private ear ;
Scare not the crowd with omens.

PRIEST.

O great King.
May heaven avert such omens from thy head,
And from thy people !

ADMETUS.

What's the matter now,
That it hath set thee gasping, like a calf
Hurt with the steel of death ?

PRIEST.

O, my good Lord,
The image of the god—

ADMETUS.

Well, hath it spoken,
That thou should'st look so ghastly ?

PRIEST.

Nay, my Lord,
The oracle hath spoken.

ALCESTIS.

And spoken ill ?

ADMETUS.

What of this image, and this oracle?

PRIEST.

Even as we waited for the virgins' song,
Bright herald of thy coming, this wan gloom
Came creeping o'er the temple ; and thereon
A moaning wind from the oracular cave
Swept through the house of the god, and reft away
The linen veil, thine own revealing hand
Should shortly have withdrawn ; and, like the sun
From out a cloud, that wonder dawned on us ;
But it wept tears of blood !   The gory drops
Stained the fair ivory cheeks, and heavily
Fell in warm rain even to the sandalled feet,
Curdling upon the marble pedestal.

ALCESTIS.

What may this mean?

ADMETUS.

What says the oracle?

PRIEST.

My tongue scarce dares to phrase it, uttering ill.

ADMETUS.

My ear dares hear what ill thy tongue can utter.

PRIEST.

Sinew thy heart to hear ; for death is dreadful.

ALCESTIS.

Death !

ADMETUS.

      Ha ! thy word, it seems, imports my death.
If so, speak plainly.

ALCESTIS.

          Death !

PRIEST.

                Thy death, O King !

ALCESTIS.

O no, no, no ! mine, mine, or any one's,
So not the King's ! This oracle, whose voice
We have waited, as a mother for her babe's,
To murder us thus ! Will the just gods so blast
The hope of the young world? O not the King's !
Thou hast mistook, old man.

PRIEST.

Alas ! dear Lady,
Would that it bore mistaking ! When the Fates
Cast up their doom, not Zeus himself shall dare
To meddle with their mind ; and now, even now,
Stern Atropos, with dull averted eyes,
Opens all wide the inexorable shears,
Which closed shall cut Admetus' golden thread.
Two hours before yon mourning orb goes down,
Thy life must stagnate in a three days' trance,
Which only death shall end. Thus saith the oracle.
So my black news is told.

ALCESTIS.

O I grow faint !
[*She faints.*

ADMETUS.

Thy news has killed my Queen before myself.
Go some of you and fetch my chariot here,
To bear her to the palace. Sweet Alcestis !
Rise up, my love, and help thy Lord to die.
Go thou, see to these rites—what ceremonies
May fitly be performed, perform. The games
Shall hold, though I die viewing them. [*Exit* Priest.

Alcestis!

Heart of my life, look up! Day's blessed star
Comes flaming forth once more, and tenderly
Kisses thy clustering tresses. O, for shame,
To lose one moment of this latest hour
That we may live together!

ALCESTIS.

Ah! too weak,
Too weak to be thy wife! This sudden woe!
What shall I do for thee?

ADMETUS.

Be strong, be strong!
Help me to die as doth befit a king;
And reign thou in my stead. 'Tis hard to bear
This envy of the Fates. Twelve years, twelve years!
And I had smiled in Hades' wintry eyes,
Leaving a nation fledged, a sceptre firm
In my son's capable hand; but now I feel them
Chill, chill; but 'tis not fear. I trust Eumelus
For noble nurture to the gods and thee.
All may be well without me. We're grown old,
And ripe for death, when we consign the world
To wreck without our steering.

ALCESTIS.

My fair world
Is wrecked already.

ADMETUS.

Nay, not wrecked, not wrecked—
Dear, I have much to say and much to do,
Ere this sun set—of minutes to make hours.

ALCESTIS.

Is there no hope in heaven? O bright Apollo,
Is there no hope!

ADMETUS.

None, none what should there be?
Poison me not with hope, nor drug thyself.
To business, come! I must dismiss this crowd
That stares and wonders still. O, ye Pheræans,
Let calm words calm the trouble of your minds!
Behold how faithfully the genial sun
Has kept my promise, and through cloudless heaven
Showers twofold radiance from his golden wheels!
The flocks again feed tranquilly; the lark
Mounts with a blissful hymn; and will your veins
Hold longer than these creatures' of the field

B

The ice of a vain fear?   Shout to your god
Harmonious greeting !   Form your ranks again,
And onward to the temple.   Come, your hymn !

HYMN TO APOLLO.

When from the splendours of thy heavenly home
   Thou didst descend, great Lord of life and light,
To make our vales thy dwelling, and to roam
   After the wandering flocks whose fleeces white
Were sage Admetus' treasure ; thou didst bind
   Our souls to thee with gentle services ;
      For, under shadowy trees,
When covert cool thy faltering charge would find
   From sunburnt noon, while in the glowing leas
The shy mole-cricket shrilled, our ardent youth
   Would circle round thee, lad and shepherd lass,
   Sitting at ease or couched upon the grass,
And drink thy words, fresh well-heads of sweet truth.

Then haply thou wouldst take thy lyre and sing
     Unto the listening ring
August Olympian idylls, that would charm
   From the wild glens some wondering wild thing.
The tenderest virgin had no thought of harm
   When from the steep gorges of Othrys came
   Lynxes, with slouching steps and eyes of flame,

To coax with furry flatteries her white arm ;
    Or spotted pards grown tame
Would push against her newly-budded breast,
    - Purring to be carest.

The ewes new-shorn, would calmly chew the cud,
    And watch the nibbling of their half-grown lambs,
    And sleepily would stare the lordly rams
'Neath their horn'd foreheads, when fell beasts of blood,
Grey forest-wolves, in shamefaced innocence
    Would lie down with the flocks, lolling to cool
Their bloodless tongues, like shepherd's dogs ; immense
    Uroxen from the mountains in some pool
Of the still stream with our tame herds would stand,
    Lashing their lazy tails ; and dappled fawns,
    On springy pastern bounding o'er the lawns,
Would munch the apple from a maiden's hand.
    When thou didst set our hills and valleys ringing
    With thy sweet singing.

O king of shepherds, shepherd of each king
    Of soul-awakening song ! Thou who didst make
This land of ours, by thy blest sojourning,
    Dear as the wandering isle where thou didst wake
To glorious life, be still propitious ! Be
    Still to this soil of bards what the young sun

Is to the earth—a luminous soul, a sea
  Of glowing beauty—life and light in one !
O Lord Apollo, bright-haired king Apollo,
Whose feet serene the mighty Muses follow,
  By thy keen shafts, and thy victorious bow,
      Which smote thy reptile foe,
  And by thy crown of healing, be our aid
Against all reptile powers that make high hopes afraid ;
  Make evil things to crouch, like a hound smitten,
    Or a tamed tiger-kitten ;
  And when despondency's chill clouds invade,
  O bid our souls fly sunward, like the swallow,
      Benign Apollo !
  [*Exeunt* Youths *and* Maidens *processionally, singing.*

ADMETUS. (*to crowd*)

Follow the singers, friends.   What now the gods
Reveal imports no danger to the state.
I am your bulwark, and what falls on me
My shoulders can sustain.   A brief farewell ;
We meet you at the arena.   Come, my love !
                     [*Exeunt.*

Scene II.—The slopes of Mount Œta, on the borders of
Thessaly. Enter ÆGLE, following her goats.

ÆGLE.

Roam as ye will, unruly beasts of mine—
I'll climb no further for you. O for the rod
With which Apollo charmed the wandering flocks
Of good Admetus ! But poor mortals ever
Must take mere mortal trouble. I'll stand here,
On this sea-gazing crag, and let the breeze,
Fresh from the kiss of blue Ægean waves,
Play in my bosom. Ha ! thou unmannered thing,
Wilt thou unbind my hair ? Here, take it then,
And let it stream upon thee, wild and free,
As any nymph's of Dionysus' train—
I'll be Athena's mænad. Beautiful !
Let poets sing of Tempe ; to my thought
This is the loveliest vale of all the earth.
There sleeps the Malian gulf no storm can rouse,
So close Eubœa folds it ; to its breast
Leaps bold Spercheius from his rocky bed,
Crowned like a bard with laurels, fairer than
Those which they say do cluster round the head
Of Daphne's Peneus ; far across the vale,

Where in the sun I see my mother's cot,
Ringed with its corn and olives, his hoar snows
Gleam o'er the pines of Othrys.   Beautiful !
Such sun and air make me intoxicate
With a strange passion—joy, is it, or pain?
Or mingled both?   O to abandon me
To some o'ermastering power, as to this wind,
Till it were joy to die for 't !

[*Voice heard singing :*

I.

Roaming through a forest-glade,
   Alack the day, alack the hour !
Love loosed on me a pretty maid,
   To fool my heart into his power.
Nay, nay, my heart's asleep, quoth I :
   Lullaby, O lullaby !

2.

But surely I was overbold,
   Alack the hour, alack the day !
For I grew hot, though she grew cold,
   And my poor heart was stolen away ;
And all in vain I sit and sigh :
   Lullaby, O lullaby !

ÆGLE.

                              What comes here,
Striding the crest of Œta like a bull,
And bellowing gentle music?   On my word
If labouring earth would find a droning-pipe,
To bear a cheerful burden, this were he!

                              [*Enter* Hercules.

HERCULES.

Whom have we here?   A nymph, gracious and tall,
And kilted short for climbing!   What art thou?
An Oread of these mountains, or the fruit
Of a fair mortal mother by some god?

ÆGLE.

No Oread, sir; nor fathered by a god;
But a mere maiden, whom Evadne bore
To dead Alcander in yon vale.

HERCULES.

                    What vale
Breeds such mere maidens?

ÆGLE.

                    These are Œta's slopes,
And yonder plain our dear Thessalian land.

HERCULES.

Ha! Thessaly! I am in Thessaly?

ÆGLE.

But now; yon ridge parts us from Phocis.

HERCULES.

'   Tell me,
Reigns King Admetus still? Is he well? Prosperous?

ÆGLE.

Even as the favourite of the gods. Thou know'st
him—
And lovest; for thy face glows at the tale
Of his well-being.

HERCULES.

Ay, I should know him well,
And love him well. The man was my dear comrade,
In deeds done in the world ere the world's eye
Was gladdened by thy face; but the world wags,
And we change favours, till the trustiest friends,
Who were more close than brothers, may pass by
Like maskers cloaked. Yet I should know Admetus.

ÆGLE.

Thou should'st be some great hero, by thy port ;
And by thy club, and by thy lion's skin,
I guess thee Hercules.

HERCULES.

Even he.   Why laugh'st thou ?

ÆGLE.

I know not why I laugh.   May one not laugh
And know no reason for it ?—Yet—I think—

HERCULES.

What dost thou think ?

ÆGLE.

That 'twas to hear a song
So tame, from a so mighty throat.

HERCULES.

O ho !
What ailed the song ?

ÆGLE.

Pshaw ! 'twas a paltry song—
A milk-and-watery song. To hear the thunder
Intone a babyish lullaby ! O ye gods !

HERCULES.

Well, young one, laugh thy fill. What is thy name?

ÆGLE.

Ægle.

HERCULES.

A sweet name—bright and gracious—Ægle !
A nymph-like name ! So, thou'rt a judge of singing?

ÆGLE.

O, I have heard my grandsire, old Chrysippus,
Hymning the gods in such immortal strains
That I have wept to hear him. I have stood,
Tranced like a bird asleep in the air, while he
Hath sung me tales of old heroic deeds.
Thou wilt have heard his name? He is a bard
Thrice crowned ; and this same day he will contend
Before Admetus, at Apollo's games,
With all the bards of Greece. My mother needs me,

Or I had seen this festival—O the bliss
To hear them sing!

HERCULES.

Would'st thou not see them run,
And wrestle, then?

ÆGLE.

That too; but O the singing!
To see my grandsire crowned! I have offered daily
The laurels of our vale to King Apollo,
Bright with his Daphne's tears; have gathered for
The Muses pensive pansies—save for her,
Whose lyric breath makes musical the heart
Of the lorn nightingale, Calliope,
Whom most our bards invoke. Her I have wooed
To be propitious with the sweetest flower
That breathes its soul in the woods, the violet—once
Dimmed with the blood of Orpheus, her great son,
When the mad Mænads tore him.

HERCULES.

Meetly done;
But I would see these games. How far to Pheræ?

ÆGLE.

Three days a-foot. Thou art too late. Three days
The games will hold, no more.

HERCULES.

Yet I'll push on—
It lies upon my way—and see Admetus.

ÆGLE.

Would I were free as thou ! I saw him once—
'Twas when he made procession through the land,
To test his people's thriving. But that his head,
A little bent, for thought, and some sad lines
About the mouth and eyes, proclaimed him mortal,
He might have been Apollo's self come down,
To heal the suffering world—stern and yet loving,
A radiant awe, not terror. Why art thou
Not awful, yet a hero?

HERCULES.

Why art thou
Not bashful, yet a maiden?

ÆGLE.

Nay, I know not.
But O the Queen !

HERCULES.

Alcestis ! sawest thou her ?

ÆGLE.

Ay, she was with him.   Her divinest face,
Where love lay fathomless in beauty's deep,
Gave me dim eyes and choking at the throat,
As noble deeds do chanted.   To meet her look,
Sad as Demeter's with its weight of love,
Was to grow pure ; the melody of her smile
Was silent blessing.   I was never rich
In happy thoughts of life till I saw her.

HERCULES.

Why 'tis a peerless Queen !   I'll to the court,
And see its jewel, though I take no prize.

ÆGLE.

Thou would'st have wrestled shrewdly, though for
    singing,
Zeus framed thee not.

HERCULES.

Wert thou the wrestler's prize,
Methinks these arms could wrestle with the best.

ÆGLE.

I am no prize for wrestlers, Hercules!
Rate me not thus, a free Thessalian maid,
With captives and barbarians. Thou growest fond!

HERCULES.

Thou'rt a strange girl. Alack! the best of us
May Zeus unstate. But the bright day grows old—
I'll seek some harbour in yon vale of yours,
And food withal, and wine.

ÆGLE.

                    I'll be thy guide.
My mother loves not strangers; but for thee,
Admetus' friend, the best of what we have
Will be thy least of welcome. Thou shalt taste
The vintage of our valley. As we go,
Tell me, I pray, thy labour ended last,
And what thou goest to now.

HERCULES.

                    Both lightly told
The Cretan Bull's in Argos; and I go
To drive away the steeds of Diomed
From Thrace.

ÆGLE.

What are those steeds?

HERCULES.

For oats and hay,
They munch up men, I'm told.   Strange things I've
    seen,
But these not yet.

ÆGLE.

Alas! what things there be
In this bright world! Thee, too, they will devour.

HERCULES.

I hope not.   Wilt thou shed a tear for me,
If I be eaten?

ÆGLE.

Tears are precious pearls—
I've none to grace thy pall.

HERCULES.

If thou'lt not weep.
I'll not be eaten.   Come, I grow so hungry
That I am tempted sore to eat thyself—
Thou art but a mouthful for me.

ÆGLE.

                    Heaven forefend !
Thou'rt a most dangerous monster.   Follow me down !
A kid shall be my ransom from thy jaws.

                                   [*Exeunt.*

────

Scene III.—Temple of Apollo.   Enter ALCESTIS and
          EUPHRANOR, meeting.

ALCESTIS.

The King's in deepest trance !   At last I come,
A suppliant, as thou see'st, from tendence on him
Most miserably freed—wearier than all
My worn-out messengers.   Once more I'll rack
Thy tortured ear : O, is the oracle
Still dumb ?

EUPHRANOR.

                    Still dumb, O Queen !   The Pythoness
Still sleeps ; and none dare break her rest.

ALCESTIS.

Still dumb !

Were all the lustral rites performed?

EUPHRANOR.

All, Madam.

The sacred virgins led her secretly,
In silence, to the deepest cavern, where,
Still fasting, her chaste body in the brook
Seven times she laved ; then, donning her white stole,
She plucked three leaves from great Apollo's tree,
And chewed them ; and with nine her head she crowned ;
But ere she touched the tripod fell this sleep
From heaven upon her eyes.   The virtuous boughs
Of our unfading laurel, whispering still
With each oracular air the cavern breathes,
Bend o'er her rest.   If her pale lips but move,
A hierophant stands by to note it.   Madam,
I pray your patience ; for I grow to think
Some great deliverance will be wrought.

ALCESTIS.

O thanks !

For any word of comfort take my thanks !
But go thyself into the inmost shrine—

c

Note her thyself.   Alas ! I am grown mad,
And would importune Zeus, or Death himself,
Or the unyielding Fates, to medicine me
With hope, as dying men clutch bitterest balms.
Have pity on thy Queen, and go once more !
I'll kneel and wrestle here till I drop dead,
Or win some comfort—go !

EUPHRANOR.

Dear Queen, I go.
Would I were Zeus, so I might staunch with joy
The fountains of thine eyes.

[*Exit* Euphranor.

ALCESTIS.

O kind Apollo !
Who didst so cherish us once, wilt thou forget
Admetus now, when not to succour him
Were but to blight thy favour's opening May
With a thrice-bitter frost ! Thou who dost know
Thyself both love and tears, who owest Death
Many a deep grudge, look now upon our love,
Which soared its lark-like flight, a mounting hymn
In thine own praise, struck bloodily in full song
By this most cruel hawk.   What tower of crime
Can any god o'erturn upon the head

Of this, thy friend, save too much trust in thee?
O save him now, and save thy glorious name
On the warm lips of men, thy holiest praise
In their adoring hearts!

> [*Re-enter* Euphranor.

What now?

EUPHRANOR.

O Queen,
The Pythoness hath spoken in her trance,
Marvellous things! Apollo stands before
The never-lifted veil; his radiant self
An earnest-pleading voice.   He's dumb but now,
While the all-dreaded Three, in silence dread,
Look in each other's eyes, to read the doom
Of thy great consort.

ALCESTIS.

Silence guard my life
From sinful thought in this grim hour of doom!

> [*A pause; then enter a Priest suddenly.*

ALCESTIS.

O, is there help in heaven?

PRIEST.

Ay, help in heaven,
So there be help on earth.

ALCESTIS.

What dost thou mean?

PRIEST.

Admetus lives, if there be found a friend
To die for him.

ALCESTIS.

To die for him? A friend?
Must then some man, or may a woman die?

PRIEST.

A man or woman, Madam.

ALCESTIS.

Gentle Fates,
I thank you for this doom! He's saved! he's saved!
[*Exit* Priest.

EUPHRANOR.

Alas! what means this sudden ecstacy?

ALCESTIS.

My Lord is saved !

EUPHRANOR.

How saved? Will any die
To save his friend? Yet for the King we'll make
All proclamation—

ALCESTIS.

Proclamation, man !
What proclamation? Who should be his friend,
But I—his wife ?

EUPHRANOR.

Thou ? Thou wilt die for him !
O prodigy of love !

ALCESTIS.

No prodigy,
Save love's a thing prodigious—love that lives
By looking in death's eyes. Will soldiers die
For hate, and wives not die for love ? Will men
Hold their lives cheap, and risk them every day
On perilous seas, high scaffolds, in dark mines,

For a poor piece of bread ; in games, brawls, battles,
For praise, gain, duty ; and shall women fear
To die for love's sweet sake ?   O where's the wife,
That mounts the nuptial bed, but ere she sees
The darling first-born face outfaces death
In the warm nest of love?   I die to-day—
I might have died to-morrow, when my death
Gained no great life for the world.   Admetus lives :
I triumph over death in this strong son
I bring again to mightier birth.

EUPHRANOR.

O, Queen,
Thy words are as a wind that bows my head
In trembling awe !   My life is but a reed,
Shaken, astonied, fluttered.   I am not
The stolid thing I was.   What can I say?
O let me kiss thy feet !

ALCESTIS.

Stand up, stand up !
Kneel to the gods, not me.

EUPHRANOR.

But let me still
Make proclamation.

ALCESTIS.

     Ay, proclaim the doom—
Say not a word of me—we'll test the love
Of all this people. What if they come in crowds,
Clamorous for death, to put their Queen to shame—
How wilt thou hold me then?

EUPHRANOR.

     Not less their Queen.

ALCESTIS.

Farewell till then.

EUPHRANOR.

     Farewell, O peerless wife!

End of Act First.

ACT II.

Scene. I.—Pheræ—a Street. Enter a CITIZEN and a SAILOR.

CITIZEN.

They say the King must die.

SAILOR.

Die? Ay, we must all die—kings and cow boys, princes and pettifoggers, we must all one day tussle for stowage-room in old Charon's cargo.

CITIZEN.

But this is death upon strange conditions—thou hast seen the proclamation?

SAILOR.

Ay.

CITIZEN.

Then here's a chance for thee: to die and save the King ! How often hast thou pulled death by the beard upon mean occasions, and this would be thy immortal honour—a statue of gold to thee, and wealth to thy posterity. Thou shouldst have a talent in thy hand, to drink such a rouse with father Charon that he would clap thee on the back, and ferry thee over Styx in the barge he keeps new-cushioned for demi-gods. What sayest thou?

SAILOR.

I had rather be chained to the rowers' benches of this good ship Life. For the statue of gold, its gleam would send small candlelight of honour into the nether darkness; and for my posterity, they are so scattered over this wench-bearing earth that they are beyond knowledge of their roving ancestor. Grant me to live till I can bring my family within the castigation of a single rope's end, and I will die for the King, and welcome. But just now I am in no dying vein. Since Admetus beached the Tisiphone, my old war galley, I have no business with death. Go die thyself, man. The King will father thy children, and thou may'st reign in Hades.

CITIZEN.

Better be a farmer's slave in Bœotia. Besides it would smack of presumption in me to call myself the King's friend.

Sailor.

I marvel how the Queen can be so fond as to make
this proclamation. A man will face some smart
chance of death, d'ye see, in the rash heat of
life—for his own sake, for his private ends, renown,
or duty, or mere love of danger. He would be no
man else. But die for another in cold blood—no,
by Hercules, not I! But should not old Pheres be
content, think you, to hide his palsied head, at this
hour of the day, and for his son?

Citizen.

Not he; not he; why, the old cling to life as men
sliding over a precipice to every bush. They drop
into the grave with its rotten twigs clutched in their
feeble fists. No, *he'll* not die.

Sailor.

But what of his mother, Clymene?

Citizen.

The mother's love, says the saw, thins with the
mother's milk. Their embrace is life to us at first:
but at last the narrow gripe of their kindness would
strangle us.

SAILOR.

Or the Queen Alcestis?

CITIZEN.

Her children will cause the perdition of their father, weighed in an even scale. Trust me, I know the appetites of these women. They hold us mere appendages of our children, once we are fathers.

SAILOR.

You think so?

CITIZEN.

I know it, by Zeus! and to my cost.

SAILOR.

Then farewell, poor Admetus! Hath he no mistress, who in the first heat of her affection might e'en die for him?

CITIZEN.

Not one sweet morsel of Aphrodite's flesh; the chaste husband of a chaste wife—they tell me.

SAILOR.

A wonder among kings! How many men in his place would now so dangerously hang by a single woman's hair!

CITIZEN.

One of his royal whims, sir—peace be with him!

SAILOR.

A king to be more constant than a god!

CITIZEN.

Or a sailor—eh?

SAILOR.

But this queen of his might fix the wandering fancy of Zeus himself?

CITIZEN.

A paragon, a paragon! Shall we go? Business must march, though monarchs die.

SAILOR.

Well he was a good king, say I—always stirring— his sails are on all seas.

CITIZEN.

A good king, as kings go, I grant you; but full of notions—a meddler with old customs—a bringer in of strange cattle.

SAILOR.

What, Apollo's sheep?

CITIZEN.

Ay, sir, I remember our old mountaineers. I have dealt in wool myself in my day. These sheep of Apollo's breed will shew you a heavy fleece, a fine long-stapled wool—I grant you that; but they are given to the rot beyond all beasts of their kind.

SAILOR.

Is that so?

CITIZEN.

Most certain. Come, I can tell you more secrets than this.

[*Exeunt.*

Scene III.—Nuptial Chamber of ALCESTIS. ADMETUS in his
trance. Enter ALCESTIS.

ALCESTIS.

The hour approaches. Dear my Lord, I come
To break thy three days' trance. Thou mighty dæmon
Of love, whom, trembling at the gloomy gate
Of Hades' realm, I once had vision of,
Sustain me now ! O give me back the glow
Of self-devoting rage, that made the pangs
Of death so died seem life's last ecstacy !
I am filled with fighting since—a pent-up storm,
A fire beneath my snow. The rebel brood
Of solitary thoughts have torn my breast,
Crying against the unjust decrees of heaven
That puff away my life ; for, not to die—
Pah ! the vile thought but whispered in my soul
Were tenfold death. While thou liest there, my dear,
And I stand here, that thought can never rise ;
No, though the tender arms of dearest hopes,
Cling round my neck soliciting me. Now
Admetus, take my life, from lips more fond
Than were thy virgin bride's, which press to thine
This more than nuptial kiss !

          [*Kisses him. He wakes.*

·ADMETUS.

                Do I still dream?
Methought I waited by the gloomy coast,
For Charon's dismal ferrying, till there came
A winged thing, and rapt me home again.
Mine eyes are dim; but art not thou Alcestis?

ALCESTIS.

I am, I am! O my most dear Admetus!

ADMETUS.

My true Alcestis! What, am I restored
To thee and the world?

ALCESTIS.

           Thou hast thy life once more,
To make a stair of perdurable deeds,
By which the world shall mount.

ADMETUS.

             Ha! then the gods
Bear us some love indeed. Life, blessed life!
How fresh thy fields look now, to one returned
From a so perilous voyage! My Alcestis,

Thou art my saviour; thy prevailing prayers
Have been as gentle winds to waft me back
To thy sweet bosom.　Thou didst smooth my way
To bitter death; be then this holier life
All dedicate to thee.

ALCESTIS.

　　　　　　　　　　Nay, dearest, think
Of other claims than mine.　Thy people hang,
As mellowing grapes upon a vigorous vine,
On thy rich life; thy children grow from thee
Like tender suckers—and a day may come
When thou must be their mother.

ADMETUS.

　　　　　　　　　　Never dawn

A day so drear !

ALCESTIS.

　　　　　　　　　My root, like thine, may be
Untimely nipt.　Last night I saw a star,
Bright as the brightest orb that rides in heaven,
Leap suddenly into darkness.

ADMETUS.

                Slay me not
Once more with evil boding.   Be to-day
A festival of life.

                  [*Enter* Euphranor.

EUPHRANOR.

          All hail, great King !
Long may'st thou live the favourite of the gods !

ADMETUS.

Welcome old friend.   Am I not much beholden
To this sweet pleader's prayers ?

EUPHRANOR.

              Thou art indeed
But I come now, the herald of a crowd
That waits without to see thee, thus restored.
Wilt thou not show thyself ?

ADMETUS.

           Ay, with glad heart
That I am here to show.   Come, my Alcestis !

D

ALCESTIS.

Grant me a moment's pause.   I have a word
For this kind ear.

ADMETUS.

    Well, then, be brief, be brief !

        [*Exit* Admetus.

EUPHRANOR.

As jocund as the morning !   Knows he naught ?

ALCESTIS.

What hand will dare to stab him ?   Would that all
Were done, and this could hide unknown, unsaid·!
Death were no dying then—I tremble now
As though I did some crime.   When shall I die ?

EUPHRANOR.

Alas ! sweet Queen—

ALCESTIS.

    My hour-glass is run out ?
'Tis better so—no more delays.   The thing

Is fixed, irrevocable?   Nought *he* can do
Will thrust me back on life, while he expires?

EUPHRANOR.

Nothing.   No second compact holds with Death.

ALCESTIS.

I thank the gods for that!

> [*Re-enter* Admetus.

ADMETUS.

                      Still in close talk!
Come, dearest, come; the people wait for thee,
With such a light of gladness in their eyes
As might make flush a monarch's dying face
With pride to have lived.   What, tears?   O shame,
   my love!
On such a day!

ALCESTIS.

                    Forgive me, my dear Lord,
My nerves are shaken.   O I cannot face
This shouting crowd!

ADMETUS.

                  One moment.   To refuse

The pledge of such a love were churlish.

ALCESTIS.

                                                    Well,
One moment, for love's sake.
                    [*Exeunt* Admetus *and* Alcestis.

EUPHANOR.

With what a sweet and melancholy grace
She bears this pinch of torture !   In that pale
And martyred face, where pain itself becomes
An aureole of more tenderness, and makes
Beauty twice beautiful, I see the soul
Of womanhood incarnate.   Strange, most strange,
That when strong men but rage and curse, weak women
Will smile and bless—'tis strange!   Well, pain and death
Are mysteries of the gods ; but such a face
Is as an azure glimpse of ether, seen
Above dark storms that shake the mountain-tops.
I can but weep and bow.   O gentle Queen,
Lady of sorrows, how I worship thee !
                    [*Re-enter* Admetus *and* Alcestis.

ADMETUS.

This is no common weakness.   On my life,
There's something hidden here !   I charge you both

By your allegiance, speak! Why do ye glance
Each at the other in a furtive fear?

EUPHRANOR.

O King—

ADMETUS.

            Can there be yet a woe so dire
Its face should make me blench?

EUPHRANOR.

            Thou knowest, O King,
Thy life, in forfeit to the Fates, was spared—

ADMETUS.

Ay, at her intercession.

EUPHRANOR.

            O, my Lord
Apollo's self, a suppliant at their throne,
As none before, could barely wring from them
This boon, upon condition—

ADMETUS.

            Ha! condition?
Will the great gods be factors for their favours,
And have their usury? What condition?—come!

EUPHRANOR.

That one should die for thee.

ADMETUS.

That one should die!
What, life for life?   O monstrous; I'll not set
My seal to such a pact!   And yet—I live—
What have ye made of me?   Who's slain for me,
While I stand chattering?

ALCESTIS.

None is slain—be calm.
A soldier dies for thee, more cheerfully,
Out of pure love, than ever on the field
He had died for duty.

ADMETUS.

Duty?—love?—a soldier?
My brain begins to swim.   Thou, thou, Alcestis,
Deny, for love's sweet sake, that thou hast stabbed
So horribly at my soul.   Thou hast not played
The whore with death? Thou'rt pale, but thou'rt
        not weak.
Thou breathest, speakest, movest—never fairer—
And thine eye sparkles, thy pulse plays, thy hand—
That's cold—that's cold—

ALCESTIS.

> O look not in my face
> With such a piteous rage !   Ah ! dear, what soldier
> Should claim to die for thee from me, thy wife,
> Thy own true, loyal, and much-loving wife,
> To whom thy death were tenfold death?

ADMETUS.

> And I,
> Have I no voice in this?   It shall not be.
> I who had died with honour, to drink out
> The dregs of a mean life—the mock of men—
> A craven vampire of the dearest blood
> Of earth's most noble veins!   I trusted thee
> Beyond all trust ; and thou betrayest me thus,
> To a base fall.   Is this thy love to me,
> Or a most cruel wrong?   It shall not be.
> I fling their boon back to the envious gods,
> And count death luxury.

ALCESTIS.

> It is too late.
> My choice is made, and ratified above,
> By those who change not twice.   O pardon me
> This sin of my love—break not this dying heart

With thy reproachful eyes ! 'Twas not thy wont
Under the guise of tender care for me,
To be the jailor of my happiness,
Like husbands I have known.   O play not now
The loving tyrant !   Count the deed as done,
As, ill or well, 'tis done ; and done so simply,
In such a frank outleaping of the soul,
That I have happy confidence it is blest
With sanction of the gods.

ADMETUS.

                         The gods ! the gods !
Name not these gods to me ! O for a curse,
Direr than death—a Titan, to drag down
The dark, almighty, and iniquitous power
That plagues the world with evil ; for a chain,
Stronger than hell, to bind him ! O that once
I might but meet him naked, man to man,
And face to face ; that my weak weaponless hands
Were at his throat !   The fury of my hate,
Which turns my blood to lava, would so steel
And sinew their tight grasp, that he should strangle,
Though all the bolts of Zeus in horrible flight
Crashed on my head at once.   What, shall we kneel,
And praise the gods, when our most innocent hopes
Are made the food for grim despair to prey on ;

When the fair smiling promises of our life,
Like child-voiced sirens, lure us to the embrace
Of perilous reefs; when love itself betrays
Our best to death and pain, and one by one
Makes bleed with torturing rods before our eyes
Our delicate-winged affections? For this boon,
What a vile mock of mercy have we here!
To rise from out the grave, its bitterness
Once tasted bitterly, and watch the face
That life alone made life become the prey
Of pale disfeaturing death! O! O!

ALCESTIS (*to Euphranor*).

                                        Go thou,
Gently dismiss the people. Say I am sick,
Or what thou wilt; and let the children wait
Here within call. Pardon me that I make
Thy goodness tend on me. And so farewell!

EUPHRANOR.

O my sweet Queen!
                          [*Exit* Euphranor.

ALCESTIS.

                    Admetus, hearken to me—
To the last words that ever I may speak.

Thou taughtest me to die, let me teach thee
To live—that's harder.

ADMETUS.

                 I'll not live !   If still
Death leaves me drugs, steel, water, in the world,
That speedily will end me?

ALCESTIS.

                 O for shame !
Can such a soul as thine, so firm and pure,
That like a noble column it upheld
The temple of thy time, be grown so weak
That this poor shock will shatter it?   Then farewell
The hopes of lost mankind !   Wilt thou so let
Self-pity's weeping mist extinguish all
The field of wholesome life?   Think of thy children.

ADMETUS.

My children—Oh !—I had forgot them.   Ay,
Let them die too—now, ere they know the taste
Of heaven's bleak tender mercies !   Let the race
Of miserable men, sickened with tears,
Go to the rest of Hades, and contend
No more with the strong lords of life !   Our backs

Are broken with their bounties.   We are crushed
Like flowers in eager children's glowing hands,
When most they favour us.

ALCESTIS.

Alas ! thy words
Are like the angry and rebellious tears
Of children—reckless and most profitless.
My dearest husband ; thou who wast to me
The rock to the weak clinger, fail me not
In my sore need—O be a man again,
And comfort the last glimpses of my day !
Look in my face, and see its sunset glow
Take ashen hues.

ADMETUS.

My dearest, O my dearest !

ALCESTIS.

So, thou art close to me ; and I can speak
Things in thine ear which hardly to thy face
I had dared to say.   Now, when the gloom begins
To gather round my soul, great visions come
Of new unfathomed deeps.   Night, that doth cloak
With shadowy wings the world's familiar face,
Undraws with her chaste hand the glittering veil

Of day that hid the stars. I blame thee not
For grief, who with her weeping sisterhood
Have made my home these three long dreary days ;
Nor count I sudden woe, and timeless death
Less than enormous ills ; but evil's self,
Like the chameleon, dyes its reptile form,
Colourless else, in the life-tinctured hues
Of hearts that beat beneath its wildering weight.

ADMETUS.

In my perplexèd ear thou speakest riddles.
Word it more plainly for me. I am dazed
And deafened by this stroke. Thy voice sounds far,
And hath strange tones in it, like music heard
O'er water through the night.

ALCESTIS.

                        Ah, dear ! thy grief
Lies sore upon me. Would that I could carry
Its burthen to my grave ! But thou must live
And bear this burthen bravely. What I speak,
Which now sounds thus remote, will come to thee
When I am gone, like echoes soft and clear,
To bring thee peace and trust. I am at peace,
My peace would leave to thee.

ADMETUS.

                              What peace or trust
Can live in this bad world? The grave is peace—
The gods, who mock our strife, permit none else.

ALCESTIS.

The gods reign but their day.   Hear me once more,
And let me seek to render to thine ear
The vision that I see.   Words are but dim
To paint the auroral mysteries of the dawn ;
But I would fain essay it.   Pain and death
Seem to me now but flickering shadows, flung
Athwart the mortal field by joy and life.
Look down, the shade is an abyss of gloom,
Yawning to gulf us ; but look up, we see
The sun that casts it ; and that sun is—nay,
I dare not call it Love ; yet it is love
That draws our eyes to it.

ADMETUS.

                              I hear thy words,
Their sense I cannot hear.   Vague oracles
And windy phrases cannot murder death,
And evil make no evil.

ALCESTIS.

        Nay ; but yet—
Ah, trust me, I beseech thee ! Flout not thus
My weak and fleeting words ; the images—
Vague images—of some eternal truth
Whereby we live, which else were imageless ;
But ponder well their echoes. I am set
Here on this couch of death, Death's Pythoness,
Scorn not my tripod.

ADMETUS.

       Scorn it ! O, my love,
I feed upon thy breath ! But speak to me
Some comfort for to-day—some dovelike word
Which, nestling in my bosom, may bring forth
A brood of peace, if thou would'st leave me peace.

ALCESTIS.

There weeps a human patience, with such tears
As fill the eyes of meek Apollo's flowers
What time their lord's away. Tender and true,
If I had never loved thee till this hour,
My shroud were woven of love. The sun I see,
That knows not day nor night, will rise for thee,
And shine on thee with comfort ; will transmute

The essence of thy grief to something rare
As the balsamic tears that wood-nymphs weep
When their loved pines are wounded ; to a balm
Of virtue med'cinal.

ADMETUS.

                              Thou art my balm ;
And thou art breathed into the wandering air,
That keeps no record of the sweets it steals.

ALCESTIS.

Not so ; I am a leaf that withering woos
Out of the air some subtle alchemy
Which turns decay to odour.   I will lie
Still in thy bosom, breathing sweeter balm
Than e'er I breathed alive.

. ADMETUS.

                    Vain dreams, vain dreams

ALCESTIS.

Nay, dearest, look no more into the shade,
Where the dull asp despair, the subtle snake
Rebellion, and the chill toad apathy
Perversely gender, and with venomous breath

Pollute the azure heaven.   These are the Furies
Whose fangs make evil evil.   Hope the lark,
And peace the dove, and the strong eagle love
Companion thee for ever.   In their eyes
There is no evil.

ADMETUS.

                              Would I had their eyes,
So they see truth.   Thy words are wonderful
And sweet—I see a glory in thy face
Which I must worship, though it severs thee
From my old knowledge.

ALCESTIS.

                              Dearest, such a death
Is as a second birth for thee and me ;
For me, because I rise into an air
Which else I ne'er were winged for ; and for thee,
Because that like a mother for her babe
I die to give thee life.   Thou art my child,
Pledged to live bravely for me, or I die
In vain, and Death stands victor.   Thou wilt live
As though I saw thee?   Promise me !

ADMETUS.

                              Freely, freely,—

ALCESTIS.

Nay, I do wrong to pledge thee. I demand
No stoic vows, no wild ascetic rites
Of self-repression. Be what thou hast been—
A glorious cedar, in whose fostering shade
All beauteous things may flourish, but more strong,
And richer, in the life of her whose leaves
Decay to feed thy root.

ADMETUS.

This love of thine
Is as a wind of autumn in my soul,
Destroying and preparing. I am bowed,
Moaning, before its strength, and quailing.

ALCESTIS.

Nay,

Be it unto thy heart a wind of spring,
Expanding and awaking. Comforted,
Not desolate would I leave thee—even to this:
That if, when cold I leave my nuptial bed,
As I must leave it, thou should'st find a maid,
Worthy thy love, to be—what I have been—

E

ADMETUS.

What have I done to merit this from thee?
What sacrilege were this—another bride,
To fill Alcestis' place!   O cold, cold, cold,
Shall be thy bed, till I am cold as thou!
I live but as thy freedman.   Canst thou deem
Me, who have known thy love, and loved thee—me
Thou hast saved, of such frail, tepid, amorous nature,
So impotent in passion, as to lose
Thine image from my arms, and sink upon
The bosom of some girl?   Am I indeed
So praised—and by my wife?

ALCESTIS.

                        Forgive the thought,
If such there be—there is not—in my mind,
Which wears the cloudy semblance of a doubt
Of thy heart's purity.   I doubt thee not:
I know thy love is steadfast as the star
That mariners make their lamp.   But men are men,
Adventurous sailors on the deep of life,
Achieving and acquiring, here to-day
And gone to-morrow—homeless voyagers,
Who cannot cast their anchor in some port

Of the loved past, and ride their life out there,
Content, like women.

ADMETUS.

Who has taught thee this?

ALCESTIS.

Thyself, the world, and death.   Thou art to-day
My husband ; thou wilt be my son to-morrow—
A man, to whom Alcestis is a dream,
A legend, loved but faded.

ADMETUS.

O no, no !

ALCESTIS.

'Tis but the law of our life.   A woman's love,
Being a thing of visions and surrenders,
Will live on relics, and maintain its bliss
By communing with ghosts.   A man's must have
A visible handmaid, for its daily wants
And passionate exactions.

ADMETUS.

Nay, my love !

I seem to see myself reflected here

In a distorting mirror. I have slaked
My heart's deep thirst in one so perfect draught
A second would be gall—the thought breeds loathing.

ALCESTIS.

Would I were worth such love ! It may be so ;
Yet I'll not make an idol for thy life
Of an o'erstrainéd constancy. If ever—
I do not say it will be—but if ever
The new Admetus of the days to come
Shall find a new Alcestis, who will take
My children—my one fear—into her heart
And be to them a mother, loving me
For what I have done for thee ; to such an one
Methinks I dare commend thee freely. Thou
Art mine for ever—fostered by my love ;
And I shall still possess thee in her arms,
And love her for thy sake.

ADMETUS.

      Can all the world
Produce a new Alcestis? Never, never !
Thou art a marvel—what, can love o'erfly
The walls of jealousy thus, and still be love ?

ALCESTIS.

No marvel, dear.   Thou art no vulgar man,
Nor I no vulgar woman.   Never, never
Wilt thou, who hast known my love, pollute my place
With some bold-browed adventuress, rashly clasped
Through sheer incontinence—some harlot thing
Whom their base father's haste makes step-mother
To his abandoned babes.   My motherly curse,
Could this bad dream come true, would have the power
Of searing thunderbolts to strike her dead.

ADMETUS.

And me as well.   Put by such horrible dreams !

ALCESTIS.

I have no fear of this ; nor yet that thou,
Like the vain bulk of outward-seeming men,
Wilt purchase some meek slave to tend on thee
And be thy children's mock.   Her I could hate,
Through mere excess of pity.   Thou hast loved,
And therefore thou canst love—walk freely forth
Where love shall lead thee, and return to me
Pure, by whatever path.   I have lived too long
With love myself to fear that it can stain.
It justifies its deeds, blesses, and saves.

'Tis its dull-eyed and wingless opposite,
Whose ever-smouldering torch, with ashy tip,
Kindles no flame of passion, that doth make
This world the lazar-house of joy.   Enough,
Death chides my long leave-taking.   I must kiss
My children ——

ADMETUS.

          Wilt thou go ?   O not so soon !
Not yet, not yet !

ALCESTIS.

          Alas ! I feel the clutch
Of icy hands that draw my feet away.
The cold mounts !

ADMETUS.

O great gods, thou art cold indeed !

ALCESTIS.

The children, let them come.

ADMETUS.

          They are here, they are here.
          [*Enter children, with Nurse.*

ALCESTIS.

My dearest, I must leave you.

CLYMENE.

Dost thou go
Into a trance, as father did?

ALCESTIS.

I go
A long, long journey.

CLYMENE.

Will it last three days—
Three long, long dreary days?

ALCESTIS.

I cannot tell
How long 'twill last; but thou must promise me
Thou wilt be good till I come back again,
And never vex thy father.

CLYMENE.

I'll be good.
And wilt thou bring me then some pretty thing
From the new place thou goest to?

ALCESTIS.

I'll remember
My little Clymene.   Kiss me, my darling,
And love me always.

CLYMENE.

Must thou go away?

ALCESTIS.

Yes, I must go.

CLYMENE.

So many dreadful things
Are happening now !   It used not to be so—
Long ago—when my birthday was—O mother
I'll not have my new birthday, nor be glad
Till thou art home again !   'Twould break my heart.
O come back soon !

ALCESTIS.

There, there—kiss me once more.
Farewell, my child—be good, and love thy father.
                              [*Exit with Nurse.*
And now, my son—

EUMELUS.

O mother, mother, mother!

ALCESTIS.

Ay, here's the pinch of parting.

ADMETUS.

This will break
Again my broken heart.

ALCESTIS.

My boy, my boy,
Kill me not with thy grief! Thou must be brave
And help thy father.

EUMELUS.

O, I cannot bear it!
I'll lie down, like a dog, and die!

ALCESTIS.

Nay, nay,
Live like a man—that's nobler—for my sake,
And for thy father's. He will live for thee
And Clymene; live thou for him. Farewell—

While I have strength to kiss thee, take this kiss,
And seal thyself my son, pledged to live nobly,
As though my eye were on thee.

EUMELUS.

I will, I will.

ALCESTIS.

My veins grow ducts of death.   O my Admetus,
Farewell, farewell ! My eyes are full of gloom ;
I see the dreadful river, and the barge,
Waiting my coming.

[*A pause.*

ALCESTIS.

O I am suddenly caught—
Hurried away—Farewell, farewell, farewell !—
Live in my love !

ADMETUS.

Alcestis, O Alcestis !
She hears no more—her eyes are imageless—
Her breast is cold, her lips too weak to kiss—
O, this is death indeed !

EUMELUS.

O mother, mother !

ALCESTIS.

If thou should'st see Admetus—

ADMETUS.

I am here ;

Thou'rt in my arms, my own—

ALCESTIS.

Tell him—

ADMETUS.

O, what ?

ALCESTIS.

I see Love standing at the gates of Death.

[*Dies.*

ADMETUS.

She's gone from us—she's gone, she's gone, she's gone !

EUMELUS.

O mother, mother, mother !

ADMETUS.

O, my boy,

We are companions in the dearest loss
That ever can befall ! What have we left
But in the sad remainder of our days
To live as she would have us ?   Leave me now
A moment.   My poor boy ! This binds us two
With bonds that but our sin can sunder—Go !
Thou shalt come back anon.

[Exit Eumelus.

Alcestis dead !—Is it true ?—At peace, at peace—
Thou would'st leave me at peace ! Alas ! I see
This desolation is a sort of peace.
The tempest's past—Dread calm !—Ah, cold, cold,
       cold !
No sense, no breath—thou who an hour ago
Wast my life's breath of life.   When thy heart's ice
The world should freeze.   Yet vilest things live on :
The traitorous kind live on ; old lechery
Lives on ; the wife unloved, the husband hated
Lives on ; all human nothings thrive apace :
Hate lets its votaries live, but love hath made
An ancient pact with death.   O speak once more,
And wake some faith in me !

[Enter Œnanthus.
Sirrah, what now ?

Œnanthus.

Admetus! O my sweet lady! My dear lady! O piteous sight! A heavy day for us all! This unroofs the house indeed.

Admetus.

Come, stint thy lamentation, man! What now?

Œnanthus.

Alas! my dear master, this is a blow indeed—this is a stroke indeed. But I crave pardon, I come to notify a thing unto thee.

Admetus.

What thing?

Œnanthus.

Hercules stands without, newly arrived, and would see thee.

Admetus.

What Hercules?

ŒNANTHUS.

Why, Hercules himself—the great Hercules. He
with the lion's fleece on his back, and the mighty club
in his fist.

ADMETUS.

I cannot see him now—I cannot see him now.

ŒNANTHUS.

Shall I so report thee to him?

ADMETUS.

Nay, nay—what do I say? To let grief murder
hospitality, that were not *thy* way. Say I'll be with
him straight.

ŒNANTHUS.

Ay, my Lord.

ADMETUS.

And set the banqueting-hall in order; prepare the
garlands; uncellar my choicest wines.

ŒNANTHUS.

The banqueting-hall, my Lord! Thou wilt not
drink with him—to-night—with——

ADMETUS.

Do as I bid thee—hence—I'll come to him straight.

ŒNANTHUS.

Ay, my Lord.

ADMETUS.

And light a good fire—methinks 'tis very chilly.

ŒNANTHUS.

Chilly, my lord?

ADMETUS.

Ay, is the day not cold?

ŒNANTHUS.

Nay, my Lord, 'tis warm enough—a fine warm evening, in respect of the season.

ADMETUS.

So? Then 'tis well enough—'tis well enough. And, hark thee, not a word of my trouble.

ŒNANTHUS.

No, my Lord.

ADMETUS.

We must make him welcome.

ŒNANTHUS.

Ay, my Lord.

[*Exit* Œnanthus.

ADMETUS.

Ah ! yes my love !   Thy cold lips counsel patience,
And I'll be very patient for thy sake,
And the day's work do well.   Thou art not gone.
Thou hast become a presence in my soul,
And I henceforth am dedicate to thee.

[*Exit.*

Scene III.—Before the Palace of ADMETUS.

HERCULES.

By Hera's eyes, a pleasant nook o' the world,
This nest of our Admetus !   All the long years,

That I've been vermin-killing, he's been planting
A garden for the Muses.   Well, why not?
Each man his function—so the world goes round.
This wife of his, they say, is something rare—
A thing divine ; and he a constant man—
That's rarer yet.   How many wives have I had?
All fair and—little else.   O woman, woman,
What should we be without thee ; and what things
Thy wantonness makes of us !   They are burrs not
    anchors—
They cannot hold us long.

> [*Enter* Œnanthus.

                                   Well, my good fellow,
What of Admetus?

ŒNANTHUS.

                                   He'll be here anon.

HERCULES.

You have here a pleasant site, a pleasant air.
What water's that ?

ŒNANTHUS.

                        Bœbeis Lake.

F
.

HERCULES.

Bœbeis?

A very pleasant lake—and boats upon it?

ŒNANTHUS.

Ay, sir, there be some boats. The farmers keep
Their sheep-boats on it, and the King doth keep
His boats of pleasure on it.

HERCULES.

Those are sheep

On yonder hillside? Sheep are they, or goats?

ŒNANTHUS.

Sheep, sir; there are flocks about— there are flocks
about.

HERCULES.

And cows too?

ŒNANTHUS.

Cows, sir, too—a many cows.

HERCULES.

Why this is richer than Arcadia—eh?

ŒNANTHUS.

I never saw Arcadia ; but the place
Is rich enough, for that.   Here comes the King.

> [*Enter* Admetus.

ADMETUS.

Hail to thee, son of Zeus !   Fair welcome here !
We are too long strangers, Hercules.

HERCULES.

> And all hail,
My dear Admetus !   Thy Thessalian land's
The daintiest nook of Greece.

ADMETUS.

> 'Tis well enough.

HERCULES.

But what is this ?   What means this robe of grief
Which ill becomes the sunshine ?   Thou look'st pale,
Thine eyes are red with weeping, and thy locks
Shorn—but for whom ?   If for thy father, surely
He dies at a ripe age.   Death comes to all,
And coming late's a friend.

ADMETUS.

My father lives.

HERCULES.

Thy mother, then?

ADMETUS.

Lives too.

HERCULES.

What! not thy wife?
Nay, not Alcestis?

ADMETUS.

She is very well—
I thank the gods, my wife is very well.

HERCULES.

Why then these mournful shews?

ADMETUS.

I mourn for one,
Not born within our house, and yet a friend—
A very faithful friend—a kinswoman

To whom I am much beholden.   She lived here,
Her parents dead, an orphan—

HERCULES.

                              Well, man, well,
This is a stroke of sorrow, to be sure,
Yet such as may be borne.   A little time,
And a few tears, and thou wilt laugh again.
Man was not made for grief, say I.   It eats
The sinews very shrewdly, nips the heart,
And scants the tale of daily work.   The man
Who gives the flout to sorrow is a god.

ADMETUS.

Then I'm no god.

HERCULES.

                              Thou takest it heavily
In sooth.   I would that I could cheer thee, man—
If I could slay a monster now, or crack
The ribs of some tough giant for thy sake,
I'd do it, as soon as eat ; but sorrow, sorrow,
That Hydra of the water of the eyes
Baffles my club.

ADMETUS.

> I thank thee heartily,
> And welcome thee to all the best I have.

HERCULES.

> Nay, to bring feasting to the house of mourning
> Were but a sorry trick. I'll e'en push on,
> And hope to laugh with thee when next I pass.

ADMETUS.

> By Bacchus and Demeter, thou shalt tarry
> Nowhere but here ! Admetus' doors stand wide
> To every stranger ; and for such a guest
> As Hercules their widest is too narrow.
> The banquet-hall's apart. Thou wilt not hear
> The women cry ; and thou shalt eat and drink,
> With hearty welcome, and be merry. I
> Can but set lips unto thy loving cup,
> And then must crave thy pardon. There are things
> That ask my overlooking. This, my steward
> Will give thee careful tendance. Go before
> And see the lamps are lighted.

> > > > [*Exit* Œnanthus.
> > > > Shall we in ?

HERCULES.

I trouble thee too much ; but take thy welcome
As freely as 'tis given ; for, to speak truth,
I have scarce touched bread to-day.

ADMETUS.

Then let us enter.

HERCULES.

When shall I see Alcestis?   All the land
Sings but her praises.   I am hungrier far
To see this peerless wife of thine than eat.

ADMETUS.

Well, after supper, after supper.   Come,
All's ready.   Thou must taste our wines.   Come in.

[*Exeunt.*

End of Act II.

ACT II

Scene I.—Nuptial Chamber of Admetus. Alcestis on her ... Admetus, Pheres, Chorus of Mourners.

ADMETUS.

With broken heart and withered life I come
To take farewell of thee, my gentle love.
Ah, would that now as coldly thou goest forth
From this my house unto the house of death.
There I but there I could not bear to ...
When with glad myriad bravery, and torches bright—
Smelling of joy, as these of blank despair—
I welcomed thee in triumph. I should ...
Have borne thee forth again. I ... to have died
As in sad sooth I did upon thy breast
In thy dear arms—how happily, methinks,
If I had died for thee. And now there art gone.
And I must live in the blank desolate world
Without thee, and a second time endure
The dreadful pangs of death—without thee.   O
Tis I that walk in the grave. thou livest still
My enshrined goddess 'Cruelties shall crave
Thy ... in the rarest ...

And in my chamber it shall smile my prayers
Some comfort back.

PHERES.

                         Nay, nay, my son—my son
In this excess of grief thou art to blame.
To mourn o'ermuch is hateful to the gods:
And thus to set this woman, thy good wife—
For she was good, a mine of wealth to thee—
To set this woman in a shrine, I say,
And worship her, were sheer impiety.

ADMETUS.

To mourn her overmuch. Methinks I mourn
No more at all. This funeral pageant seems
A dream—a pretty play. Do I shed tears?
I have wept away my tears—I am but a stone.
And if I please myself with passionate words
That have no passion in them—why? or did laugh
Or jest as well—would it have me dance?
          [aside]   When these
Old men will say: to mourn her overmuch.

PHERES.

Alas! my son these are unseemly words
For the sad business we are here upon.

I praise this wife of thine among the best
That men have wedded.   A chaste wife and fond
Is best of the god's good gifts ; and she was fond,
Even to the giving of her life for thee.

ADMETUS.

Ay, fond, fond, very fond—'twas a fond thing,
She did. (*aside.*) O Cerberus, what horrible thoughts
Will sorrow prompt !   If this old man had died,
Thou hadst been living now.   His curdled blood
That ran too slow to succour me, might have kept
Thy heart from freezing.   Cursed, cursed thought!
My poor fond father ! Nay, 'tis I, 'tis I,
Who have murdered thee—Alcestis, O Alcestis !
My love thy bloody instrument of death !

PHERES.

Why look'st thou so distraught?

ADMETUS.

                              O nothing, nothing !—
I have said nothing.   But I thank you all
For your condolements.   No, I'll grieve no more :
Wild rages, speculations, evil thoughts,
Despairs, self-accusations, groundless fears—
These are the brood of solitary grief.

PHERES.

'Tis wisely spoken.   Thy mother bade me hang
This garland on the hearse in sign of love.
She was a duteous daughter to us both,
A very duteous daughter—ever planning
Some comfort for our age.   Our loss looks pale
By thine, much greater; but must yet be wept
With what few tears are left in the parched wells
Of our old eyes.   Well, life is but a span,
And to have known a spirit so devout
Should make us bless the gods.   Shall they take up
The bier?

ADMETUS.

          Stay, stay!   I bade them bring me flowers.
Ay, they are here.   My darling, for thy brow
This crown of daisies and of marigolds
I have woven myself—flowers of the sun, that follow
His going with glad eyes.   So did thy soul
Ope to the light of truth, the heat of love,
With fearless welcome.   On thy gentle breast
Lie virgin lilies; odorous myrtle-buds,
Sweet as thy faith; and starry passion-flowers
That wither in the heat of their own love;
And in thy hand, for sceptre of death's realm,

Be fadeless amaranth.   Farewell, my Queen !
Would this last kiss were potent as thine own
To woo thee back to life !   Beautiful clod ;
Thy warmth I used to bear about with me,
And now thy cold I'll carry to my grave !
Take up the bier.

THRENODY FOR ALCESTIS.

Semichorus I.

O mansions of Admetus, let your stones
  Melt into tears !   O home made desolate
    Be to sorrow consecrate,
Thy nuptial hymns sistered with funeral moans !
    For the wedded are unwed ;
      Death has come, a dreadful guest,
    And left their chambers ravishèd
      Cold as Love's forsaken nest.
    All the air his presence owns,
    And the walls take ghastly tones,
    Echoing to the bearers' tread,
    As the mourners with bowed head
    Follow the best-beloved dead.
      Fare-thee-well !   From yonder shore
      Wilt thou return—ah, never more !

Semichorus II.

Fare-thee-well, no vulgar tear,
   No despairful threnody
Wail around thy sacred bier,
   But hymns divine be sung for thee,
Who diedst not as one who dies
Wearily, in ignoble wise.
From each drop of thy sweet blood,
   Noble woman, perfect wife,
Springs for us a healing bud,
   From thy grave a nation's life ;
All the gods were weak to aid,
Thou the fatal debt hast paid !

Full Chorus.

O sweetest flower of this sad world, soon perished !
   O self-devoted rose half-blown, farewell !
But thy pure fragrance shall be deeplier cherished
   Than all the sweets of summer.   Thou shalt dwell
A soul within the soul of highest song,
   A power divine ; and this rich month Carnean,
When the great moon is up the whole night long,
Shall be thy glory's festival.   Among
   The throned Immortals thou shalt have thy pæan.

Fare-thee-well, thy triumph sore,
Though thy like come never more,
Leaves the world wealthier than before.

[*Exeunt processionally, singing.*

Scene II.

Antechamber of the Banqueting Hall. ŒNANTHUS alone.

ŒNANTHUS.

I have seen here all kinds of guests, from all countries, that can be called countries, under the sun —Greek or Barbarian; but such a guest as this brawny Hercules never before. Are heroes then so much hungrier than your mere mortal, that they must fill their bellies in such unmannerly haste? Here he comes, and finds us with never a dry eye in the house —ashes at the gate, and my master in a most sweet and comely misery, as is but the due of so gracious a Queen; meets him merrily, with no comfortable trick of sympathy, no bated voice of condolence such as a friend should use; but roars him out a greeting, steps me thundering over the clipt hair on the threshold, and straight to his cups and his trenchers. Why 'twould

be ill manners in a Thracian! And there sits he
now, quaffing great healths to Bacchus, in wine un-
mixed, from ivy-wreathed cups; robbing our dead
Lady's bees to crown his bull's head with myrtle from
her garden-alley—where she used to walk of mornings,
how often! Alas, poor Queen! she'll never walk there
more, never more! Well, she was a good mistress—
she stood between us and blows. What, monster!
must I with one ear hear thee bellowing thy ribald
songs, and with the other the wailing of her death-
chant? O fie! fie! what an untutored world it is that
can breed such rudeness!

(Enter Hercules).

HERCULES.

Hallo there, old wineskin! Still in the dumps?
Come, drink a rouse with me!

ŒNANTHUS.

I am no wineskin, King Hercules, but the sober
steward of King Admetus: and I think it not seemly
to drink with thee.

HERCULES.

No wineskin, art thou not? Why, thou hast the

paunch of an old wineskin, the gait of an old wineskin, the complexion of an old wineskin. I warrant
thee a grave and steady drinker upon occasion.

ŒNANTHUS.

Sir, I thank the gods I can drink soberly upon
occasion ; but there's none now.

HERCULES.

Tut, tut, man !
     Drink a cup, and drown thy sorrow,
     Laugh to-day and weep to-morrow !
Hast thou any sorrow deeper than a wine-cup will
measure ? If thou hast I am but a fool.

ŒNANTHUS.

Truly under thy favour, King Hercules, truth may
be told in jest ; and I would in all humility request
and beseech thee, if thou wouldst fain exercise thy
voice in the way of music, to do it with a more
delicate dissipation, and confine thy *forandos* and
rolandos to the hall of banquet. This is the house of
mourning.

HERCULES.

So I will, good fellow, so I will. I come but for the
zest of thy festive company. I'll go back anon. Thy
rebuke is very just—"Truth, King Hercules, may be
told in jest." Ha! ha! ha! Well put, old festivity,
very well put. I thank thee for the royal title—why
dost thou call me King—eh?

ŒNANTHUS.

He whom Admetus thus royally entertains cannot
be less. Art thou not a king then, in some sort?

HERCULES.

Ay, my owl of wisdom, I am a wandering king—a
king of good fellows. My territory has no bounds.
Come, if good cheer be royalty, I'll crown thee a
king thyself. Drink, O King Curmudgeon! Thou
shouldst know the taste of this good wine.

ŒNANTHUS.

I'll not drink, I tell thee—not with her corpse still
warm. 'Tis not seemly.

G

HERCULES.

What corpse is this that comes between thee and thy liquor? 'Tis but a woman and a stranger. A woman gone! Bah! there are too many left, there are too many left. They buzz about us like bees. We are drugged with their honey, maimed with their stings. If there were none at all, we might sit down and weep; for without them to plague us, and set us by the ears, we should grow too soft and domestic. But what woman is this? Here, take thy drink.

ŒNANTHUS.

Well, 'tis but one cup to her memory, and that the wine be not wasted. Why, there's but one woman in the world, and she's gone out of it.

HERCULES.

Who? who?

ŒNANTHUS.

Who else but the Queen Alcestis herself?

HERCULES.

The Queen Alcestis!

ŒNANTHUS.

Ay, thou mayst well drop thy chalice and stare.

HERCULES.

Why, what a tale is this that Admetus put upon me!
Dead! the Queen Alcestis! Why have ye kept this
from me? Fool that I was! When died she, fellow?

ŒNANTHUS.

But now, an hour before sunset, even as thou
camest. The King laid it straightly upon us that we
should not tell thee ought.

HERCULES.

Ay, this is like his courtesy. Dead, dead! Alcestis
dead, and I a reveller!

ŒNANTHUS.

Yes, I saw her laid out while thou wast at table.
'Tis a most beauteous corpse—the sweetest thing, she
is, that ever gave the worms their supper. They'll
have carried her forth by this time.

HERCULES.

Carried her forth? Where?

ŒNANTHUS.

Why, to her grave.   Should the palace be polluted
all night with a body?   But thou may'st see her to-
morrow—all in fine white linen, and a posy of flowers
in her bosom—she will not be sealed up in marble for
a two days' space—a most lovely ladylike corpse.

HERCULES (*aside*).

Begone, ye idle wreaths!   Now Hercules,
If thou wouldst shew thyself the seed of Zeus
Indeed, look to thy thews.   Thou hast a deed
To do this night, shall make thy labours seem
But tiro's practice.   Now, thou pitiless thief,
Thou filcher of all beauty and delight,
I'll try for once a fall with thee !   Ay, Death,
Let me once fling these arms around thy ribs,
And I'll so maul thee that thou'lt quake for fear,
And dream of dying.   Thou shalt fly no more,
For all thy leathern wings, until thy realms
Restore Alcestis' shade.   I'll wait for him,
And catch him when he hovers o'er the tomb,
To drink the victim's blood ; or, missing that,
I'll follow him down to Hades.   Either way
Alcestis shall come back, or I no more.
Evoe ! Evoe ! to battle !

ŒNANTHUS (*aside*).

His teeth set, his eyes terrible! He's drunk, or
mad!

HERCULES.

Where is this tomb, friend?

ŒNANTHUS.

Why? What wouldst thou do there?

HERCULES.

Where is this tomb, I say?

ŒNANTHUS.

O ye great gods! Unhand me Hercules!
What have I done that thou shouldst strangle me?

HERCULES.

Her tomb, where is it?

ŒNANTHUS.

O—as thou goest by the road to Larissa. Thou
canst not miss it—just beyond the wall—a great tomb
all of marble. But wilt thou go there now?

HERCULES.

Ay, now, now, now! Out of my way, I tell thee!
Wouldst thou be flung over the house?

ŒNANTHUS.

O, mercy on us!

HERCULES.

Right or left, is it?

ŒNANTHUS.

To the right, to the right—thou canst not miss it
by this moon—a great white tomb in a grove of
cypresses.

HERCULES.

Thanks, thanks—fare-thee-well!

[*Exit* Hercules.

ŒNANTHUS.

This must be his mad fit. I have heard that all
these heroes have their mad fits. It is but a scurvy
trick for the blood of the gods to boil so in a man's
veins that it shall breed in him mere lunacy. I thank

my stars that I am yet unstrangled, and my poor
master well rid of him. A rude guest—a very rude,
rough guest! I must go see after the wine.

                    [*Exit into Banqueting-Hall.*

Scene III.—A Room in the Palace. ADMETUS alone.

ADMETUS.

No, no—it cannot be! It cannot be,
That these transcendent spirits, whose pure flame
Informs our lives with splendour, whose great thoughts
Measure the spaces of infinity,
Should be blown out like bubbles! Yet the flower
Dies in the act of seeding, in the flame
And victory of its passion ;—why not she?
Leaves she not seed behind which keeps her life?
Nay, this is true in figure, not in fact.
Creation is a stair of many steps,
Life feeding life, and life being piled on life,
In stones, weeds, reptiles, insects, beasts, and men,
Continuous, yet by leaps ; for every change,
However small's, a leap. Change—what is change?
Or permanence? This life—this permanence
In change—what is it? What am I—this self—

This passionate orb, winging infinity
With its weak pinions, memory and desire?
Say I'm myself, I know not what I say.
I live by daily dying—hour by hour
The same, yet not the same.   Shall I call the Past
My own; from which I'm driven, a shuddering thing,
By Time's stern hunting?   Or the Present?   What!
This naked moment, dead as soon as born?
That's nothing.   Or the Future, whose bright hopes
Are but as milestones on the road to death?
Yet we live somehow; and the world's a place
Where we may dream great dreams.   How shall we
      wake?
Yes, here's the question : Can we reach at last
A stage of life wherein it can put off
Its fleshly form and yet persist?   Why not?
What frames the organs by which life is life
But our own soul, or a dark something else
Which yet is soul—or what?   Yet we go out,
Like candles puffed, not willingly.   We die,
And go—ah! where?   Some say they have seen the
      dead,   .
And talked with them—tales, tales!   We have no proof
That we live on, that we shall live again.
This mocks the reach of reason.

                              [*Enter* Œnanthus.

ŒNANTHUS.

I crave thy pardon, King Admetus, in that I thus
intrude on thee, as it were in the very dull and hush
of the midnight ; but in respect of the light in thy
chamber, and that I am thy poor servant, and I
would say thy honest servant, and I would further
desire to present myself to thee in some measure of
condolency as thy—what shall I say?—what shall I
say ?

ADMETUS.

I fear, my tipsy servant. Shame, man, shame!
Well, well, what now?

ŒNANTHUS.

No indeed, my dread Lord, no indeed.   I did but
drink a drop with King Hercules, to drown grief
withal ; and I come to bring thee a cup of the same
comfort—which may now very meekly and becomingly
be done, when all's thus seemly set in order :
          Drink thy sorrow
          And drown to-morrow !
for so said King Hercules.

ADMETUS.

Set it down sirrah, and to bed with thee !

'Twould ask some cordial stronger than thy wine
To make my heart beat merrily again.
But what of Hercules?   I had forgot
His presence here.

ŒNANTHUS.

Mad, my Lord, King Admetus.   He's in his fit—
A very dangerous madman.

ADMETUS.

Mad, sirrah, how mad?

ŒNANTHUS.

I cannot say how mad he is; but very mad he is,
very mad.   If he be not stark mad, he's at the
least a homicidial lunatic—that I'll swear to.

ADMETUS.

O nonsense, fool!   But how came this about?

ŒNANTHUS.

Grief and drink, my Lord, grief and drink.   They
will turn the strongest brain.   When in his cups, he
heard tell of thy wife; for I was a little sudden with
him—I fear I was a little sudden—he rose up in a
fury, and would have strangled me in his gripe.

ADMETUS.

Strangled thee ?

ŒNANTHUS.

Ay, in good sooth. He roars at me to know where
her tomb was, and ere I could answer him I was
half-way on the road myself.

ADMETUS.

Her tomb, and why ?

ŒNANTHUS.

Ay, what I asked him, what I asked him. A very
sober, aperient question. But my belief is, under
thy favour, that he is now gone to bellow around
her tomb. 'Tis very often the manner of these
lunatics when the moon is at its full.

ADMETUS.

Pshaw! pshaw! Thou dreamest. Sleep thyself awake,
And trouble me no more. To bed, I say !

ŒNANTHUS.

But, my good Lord—

ADMETUS.

Begone, thou angerest me.   Is this a night
To plague me with such tales ?   To bed, to bed--

ŒNANTHUS.

Ay, my dread Lord—but—

ADMETUS.

Be off with thee !   To bed, to bed, to bed !

ŒNANTHUS.

      Well, my Lord—

      [*Exit* Œnanthus.

ADMETUS.

What then, can she be dead?   Alcestis dead !
That mind, which thought, which loved, which spoke
  but now,
No more than some frail quiverings of the flesh,
And ceasing with their ceasing ; or at best
A weak, sad, cowering, joyless, growthless shade
On Charon's coast—an echo of the past,
A withered leaf of life?   Nay, that's a tale
Too paltry.   If we die, we wholly die,
Will, feeling—all that delicate knot of force,

Conscious of power, we call ourself.   It may be :
The gods themselves know not their origin,
And fear their end.   If so, this life of ours,
With all its longings, strivings, hopes, and fears,
Is a poor puppet-show for each of us ;
Though for the race come some triumphant joy
Which our blind pangs prepare.   But if we live,
O we shall live indeed !   Ha ! what is this,
This glow, this hope ; this reaching out of faith,
Like babes to the breast they know not but through
    need ;
This ardour of desire, which, Pallas-like,
Through the tough sutures of cold reason's head
Leaps armed in warmer wisdom—beckoning me
From the bare known to a surmised beyond?
Do I begin to hear thy echoes, dear ?
                              [*Enter* Clymene.
What, Clymene?   My little shivering child !
How comest thou here ?

CLYMENE.

            I come to comfort thee.

ADMETUS.

To comfort me, my darling !

CLYMENE.

Mother bade me
That I must love thee while she's gone away ;
So I crept here to thee, because I know—

ADMETUS.

What dost thou know ?

CLYMENE.

I know what mother did
When thou wast in the trance.   She's gone away—
Away, away—in another bigger trance—
O, very far away !

ADMETUS.

Ay, very far !

CLYMENE.

No, no ; thou must not sigh and sit like that—
Thou must walk up and down, and wring thy hands,
And pray the gods—O—pray them very much ;
And send them things, and pray them very much ;
And then—then mother will come home again,
And I may have a birthday !

ADMETUS.

                                        There, don't cry
My little Clymene !   My little girl
We must be patient, and be very good
Till mother comes again.   We'll pray the gods
To send her soon.

CLYMENE.

                        But wilt thou wring thy hands
Enough of times ?

ADMETUS.

                        Yes, yes; now, little girl,
Back to thy bed.   Good night, my mouse, good night!
                                        [*Exit* Clymene.
O life, life, life !   Art thou a thing so dread
That we must dress thee in fantastic tales
To hide thy face from children, as in shame
We have brought them here ?   Nay, are not we our-
    selves
Children who play at phantasies?   And yet
When we essay to bare the bones of life,
Dissect our dreams, anatomise our hopes,
And carve the living heart that vexes us
With unappeased desires, thoughts infinite,

And high imaginations—what is left?
Either we are the fools of that dim power
That sends us hither, and our holiest joys—
The spiritual bread by which we live—
But painted cheats, drugs, gauds; yea truth itself
The loathsome pit of death; or these our dreams
Are glimpses, half-revealments, hieroglyphs
Of mighty meaning.   Choose: on this side truth;
On that all, all for which our spirits pant—
Dreadful dilemma !   Truth?   Nay there are truths
We dimly feel, not find.   Life must be lived
With what small daily bread of truth we are sent,
And to live well, though anguish be our drink,
Unveils Love's face.   Life somehow must be lived;
Then let us use all organs, wings as feet,
And in the light of our supremest visions
Live like immortals !

> (*Enter* Hercules, *leading in* Alcestis *veiled*).

HERCULES.

Admetus, thou and I, who have been friends,
Should meet, when we do meet, with open hearts :
Why hast thou met me like a stranger?   Why,
Being thus in trouble, hast thou coined a tale
To shut me from thy sorrow's comradeship?
Dost thou doubt my love?

ADMETUS.

No, no ! O Hercules, thou art a friend
For whom mere praise were injury ; but—

HERCULES.

But yet,
I'm a rough fellow, I'm a rough fellow—I know it.

ADMETUS.

Ay, as the fur that shakes the tempest off,
Yet keeps with tender warmth the tenderest warm.
Nay, that's not it.   But there are sorrows, Hercules,
Into whose gloom, as into death's dark wave
We must go down—alone.

HERCULES.

Looks death the darker
For the firm grip of a friend's honest fist,
To squeeze the chill off ?

ADMETUS.

Nay, but I was loath,
In the faint apathy of selfish grief
To scare thee from my door.

H

HERCULES.

And shut thy heart,
To open but thy door ! What hast thou made of me—
That I should crown my head, and feast and sing,
When she lay—To my grief I knew her not ;
But, by the gods ! for love of thee and her,
As by her praise I knew her, I'd have fought
With Death himself for her possession, man ;
Were't possible.

ADMETUS.

I know it, I know it—O speak
No more of her, no more ! I cannot bear it—
I cannot bear it now ; but take my thanks
For all thy love most heartily.

HERCULES.

Well, we'll turn
To another business I am here upon.
Thou hast been the prince of hospitable souls,
I'll tax thy kindness further ; to the bound
And circle of its utmost.

ADMETUS.

Tax it home.
What keep'st thou in the shade ?

HERCULES.

O, fair and soft!
What say'st thou to a woman?

ADMETUS.

A woman!

HERCULES.

Ay;
Whom I won lately in a wrestling-match—
A tough one too, as any e'er I played :
I feel it in my loins, back, shoulders, sides,
I warrant thee, very shrewdly.   I'd as lieve
Hold up the heavens again for father Atlas :
To crush Antæus was a joke to it.
Yet now, thou knowest, I'm on the road to Thrace,
To slay this Diomed.   I'll crave thy kindness,
That, till I come again, thou keep'st her here,
In this thy hospitable house, for me.
If I come not again, why, keep her still—
Count her thine own.

ADMETUS.

A hard thing, Hercules,
Is this thou cravest of me.   This is not seemly—

To leave thy virgin in a house of men,
Dwelling among the slaves; for what should be
The talk of me, the King, came she in here,
Like a hetaira, tended daintily,
With women at her beck?

HERCULES.

                         Faith, mostly virgins
Are frail and perishable merchandise:
But her I'll trust with anyone but thee,
And thee with her.   Come, take her at my hands;
For in sweet sooth I meant her for thyself—
To comfort thee.   For what should medicine grief
For a dead woman better than the kiss
Of just another woman, warm and living?
What sayest thou?

ADMETUS.

                    Now, by Zeus, I did not think
The man was in the world could flout at me
With such a cruel jest!   And Hercules—
The one man Hercules?   But that my blood
Is waterish all with tears, and leaves me weak,
O aspen weak!   such insult to my faith
Had waked as deep an anger.   Now I can

But stare and shudder.   Hercules? This wrong
The deed of Hercules?

HERCULES.

                         Nay, nay, believe me,
There is no insult meant thee.   Here stands one
As nobly born, as good, as beautiful,
As nobly dowered with all that gifts a wife,
As was thy dead Alcestis—worthier even
Thy most intensest love.   Take her, and prove her,
And find how true my praise.

ADMETUS.

                         O never, never!
What, in her chamber, where the air is yet
Warm with her presence; where her needle sticks,
Just as she left it, in the unfinished flower;
Where her sweet words yet echo!
O blasphemy of nature! Let me die,
Ere such ill thought can touch me!

HERCULES.

                         Time, man, time—
Time will do much.

ADMETUS.

     Ay, that is true—too true.
I am no woman whose proud folly plays
The pander to her frailty.   In my strength
I can see cracks.   I dare not play with vows,
Oaths, promises ; but if I know myself
I will dare think that, save that tender slip
Of dead Alcestis which was here just now,
My daughter Clymene, I'll have no wife
Other than her that's gone.

HERCULES.

      I give thee praise,
Right hearty praise, for thy firm constancy,
And know her worthy ; but Alcestis' self,
Did she stand here, would echo me and say
That thou did'st wrong Alcestis, spurning thus
This woman I have brought thee.

ADMETUS.

      How, how, how ?
O vex me not with riddles ! What means this
Strange iterance of an insult which doth seem
A thing far off and meaningless ?

HERCULES.

Suppose
Alcestis' self should rise from off her bier,
And claim her place—how would'st thou treat her
   then?

ADMETUS.

Alcestis' self? O dear and dreadful thought!
But that's impossible—Ah, Hercules,
Kill me not with these torturing thoughts; but rather
Stab me at once!

HERCULES.

Admetus, look on me—
Are there no traces on me of a fight
More dire than common?

ADMETUS.

Thou look'st pale and shrunk—
And—well-nigh weak!

HERCULES.

Well, to have fought with Death,
And held him, till a moment more had sent

A double monster, Hercules and Death,
To freeze in Hades—that might doubtless make
Even Hercules look weak.

ADMETUS.

What's this? What's this?

HERCULES.

Muster thy heart up for the shock of joy,
When thou behold'st the prize I won of him—
This matchless woman, whose sweet warmth, as here
I bore her in my arms, has been to me
Death's antidote.   Behold her! Dost thou know her?

[*Unveils* Alcestis.

ADMETUS.

O awful vision ! Do I dream?

HERCULES.

Hey, hey !
It seems when one's alive the other dies.

[*Seeing the cup of wine left by* Œnanthus.

What's here? Ay, wine. Come, come—off with it, man.
Drink it up quick—so—still alive it seems.
Look at her well.

ADMETUS.

                    So I do—so I do.
O this is terrible? What trick is this?
Fancy or fact? She seems to live, yet lives not.
She breathes but speaks not—stands with open eyes,
Yet sees not, smiles not—pale almost as when
She sank into my arms. This is not life.

HERCULES.

Yes, yes, she lives. Go, clasp her in thy arms;
Kiss her upon the lips, and speak to her.
See will she kiss thee back.

ADMETUS.

                    Alcestis! Dearest!
If it be thou indeed?
          [*Kisses her; she starts as from a trance.*

ALCESTIS.

                    Persephone,
August co-arbitress of Hades' realm,
I thank thee for this news.

ADMETUS.

                    What news? What news?

ALCESTIS.

That still Admetus loves me.

ADMETUS.

O, believe it !

ALCESTIS.

What should these be? They look too brave for
     shades.

ADMETUS.

'Tis I, 'tis I—O dream not thou art dead !
Thou livest, thou livest. 'Tis I, Admetus—I,
Thy husband.

ALCESTIS.

Ha ! how comest thou here? Ah me !
Art thou dead too?

ADMETUS.

No, no, I live, I live,
And thou, thou livest. See where thou art, at home.
And here stands Hercules, who fought with Death,
And rescued thee, and brought thee back to me.

O Hercules, my best friend, what shall we do
To shew our love to thee?

HERCULES.
                                    Why, love each other.
I'll seek out yon old wine-skin, your good steward,
And crave a cup of wine from him—if yet
He have not drunk all up.   Faith I'm but puny.

ADMETUS.

Do so, do so : call all the palace up,
And bid them tend on thee.   We'll come anon.
                                    [*Exit* Hercules.

ALCESTIS.

'Tis a sweet dream of home.   And may we dream
So vividly in Hades?
And I can touch thee too !

ADMETUS.
                                    Nay, this is home—
No dream of life, but very life itself.
Thy heart, like mine, beats strongly.

ALCESTIS.
                                    Life ?—this life ?
How should I be alive ?

ADMETUS.

By Death's defeat,
Whom Hercules won thee from, and brought thee back
To me,—and Clymene, Eumelus—all of us.

ALCESTIS.

Then, it is true—oh, let me think it true !
I'll pull my hair. Ha, pain ! real pain ! It must be—
That argues life indeed.

ADMETUS.

Nay, make not pain
The touchstone of true life; but bliss, but bliss,
Whereof 'tis but the shadow.

ALCESTIS (*pulling off her wreath.*)

What are these ?
A garland—marigolds and daisies ?   Flowers
Of the dear old earth ! No, 'tis no dream—Admetus !
My love !

ADMETUS.

O my Alcestis—tenfold mine
This blessed night !

ALCESTIS.

　　　　　　　　　This agony of bliss
Outrivals that of death.

ADMETUS.

　　　　　　　　　No more of death ;
Let me begin to live.　I am mad with joy,
And would do something mighty—when these limbs
Have done their trembling.　Help me then to bear
This sudden flood of fearful rapture, which
Tugs my heart tigerishly.　Tell me something
To piece our pang-rent lives.　Where hast thou been
Since we two parted?　Thou hast walked strangely far
Through the dark ways and dreadful glades of death :
What tiding or report of the Beyond
Bring'st thou ?

ALCESTIS.

　　　　　　　No more but what one newly waked
May tell of some bright dream.　Methinks I come
Back from Love's very presence.

ADMETUS.

　　　　　　　　　　To find him here,
More than a dream.　Thou art come back to me
Beautiful as a bride.

ALCESTIS.

And happier far
Than as a bride I crost thy threshold first.
O I will love thee ! Thou shalt ne'er regret
That I myself succeed myself thy bride,
And oust my own successor.

ADMETUS.

In my thoughts
I ne'er saw but thy face. Wilt thou not see
The children ?

ALCESTIS.

Let me kiss them in their beds.

ADMETUS.

Ay, better so. Clymene was here but now,
To comfort me.

ALCESTIS.

My little Clymene !
And poor Eumelus ?

ADMETUS.

Wept himself to sleep.

ALCESTIS.

He speaks not much, but loves me.

ADMETUS.

Ay, in sooth.

ALCESTIS.

He'll waken glad.

ADMETUS.

All of us waken glad
From a bad dream.   O death should teach us this :
To plant each patch and acre of our lives
With a rich seed of joy and love ; in fear,
Yet in far-reaching-hope !   I marvel now
How carelessly we crop our dearest joys,
Even in their tenderest budding; and henceforth
Each kiss of thy sweet lips shall seem a flower
Plucked for the shrine of a god, a drop of awe
Mingled with its delight.   Love should know all,
Feel all—

ALCESTIS.

And dare all.   I must kiss thee still
Though every kiss were death to me.
                                    [*Re-enter* Hercules.

HERCULES.

Good ! both
Alive, I see, and likely to do well.

ALCESTIS.
O, Hercules ! how shall we do thee good ?

HERCULES.
Get me a wife, the sister of thyself.

ALCESTIS.
That's not so hard.   Win thou the maiden's heart,
She'll be what thou wouldst have her.

HERCULES.

Nay, the heart
Needs a good head as well—both head and heart 's
Too much to win in one sweet venture—eh ?
Where grows thy compeer?   Thy good Lord, dear
        Lady,
Has had rare fortune in thee.

ALCESTIS.

Every man
Must mould his fortune found.   You shape us ill,
And blame the faults you have made.

HERCULES.

How modestly
Ye rate yourselves !   Fair lumps of passive clay,
How do you shape your shapers?

ADMETUS.

Pray you truce
To this light bickering.   Your brisk-flashing tongues
Illumine but the ripples on the face
Of the deep sea of love.   My vast content
Would take it at full tide, and plumb its depths
Where 'tis most fathomless ; would dive therein,
Drowned and yet trusting.   Such a sea is love,
That, Hercules, call for thy counterpart,
And she will hear and answer through the waves
That yearn from star to star.

HERCULES.

Pooh ! lover's dreams.
There's no such kindly and match-making sea
Pairs us like doves.   Thou hast cast a lucky line
In wedlock's ocean.   I might say to thee,
And just as truly : such a sea's the air,
That, dear Admetus, cry but for the moon,
And she will weep and flutter down to thee.

I

ADMETUS.

Maidens are gentle moons, one sweet, right word
Draws from their lonely orbits.   Still I say,
If thou art worth a wife, touch but her hand
O'er the dark gulf that severs sex from sex ;
Call her with pure desire and holy trust,
And she will come to thee.   That gulf of gloom,
Full of dark fear and ugly controversy,
Shall grow a bay of peace, a lake of joy,
A bath of new-creation, full of light,
Where ye shall live like halcyons.

> [*Enter confusedly a troop of servants, &c.*

SERVANTS.

                                    Where's the Queen ?
Where is Alcestis? Wondrous !

ADMETUS.

                                    Welcome friends !
Here stands, indeed, our Queen, come back to us.

ALCESTIS.

Yes, here I stand, alive and well, o'erjoyed
To see your joy.

ADMETUS.

               And here stand I, your King,
Blest with such love of noble wife and friend
As none e'er found before.   The gods I knew
Sat distant in Olympus in my need—
Ay, even Apollo was too weak to save.
But there's One holier, whose immortal throne's
The mortal heart—a God who died for me,
When she, my dearest, died ; who conquered death,
When Hercules triumphed.   There's no greater god
Than He whose pure and world-redeeming breath
Fills these great spirits.   Light all the palace up ;
We'll make a solemn sacrifice to Love,
Whom, as Apollo in the arts of life,
We'll worship in life's inward ways ; and then
This happy night we'll turn to happy day,
And usher in the dawn with nuptial songs.
Come, my Alcestis.
            (*Exeunt.*)

THE END.